Snoopy's Band

Rock & Roll, Country and R & B—
Snoopy's Got It All!

Based on the comic strip "Peanuts"
Created and Written by:
Charles M. Schulz

Produced and Directed by:
Lee Mendelson
Desirée Goyette

Original Music and Lyrics by:
Desirée Goyette

Music Arranged and Conducted by:
Ed Bogas

Art Director:
Frank Hill

LADIES AND GENTLEMEN. BOYS AND GIRLS... WE ARE GOING TO HAVE A SPECIAL TREAT FOR YOU TODAY. SNOOPY'S BAND IS GOING TO NEED A NEW VOCALIST. AND WE'RE GOING TO LET YOU IN THE AUDIENCE PICK THE WINNER.
WELL, I GUESS SALLY'S GOING TO START. SHE LIKES ROCK AND ROLL.
I WOULD LIKE TO POINT OUT THA PLAYING THE BASS IS MY SWEET BABBOO!!

"Don't Take Away My Rock 'n Roll"

Well, you can have all
  my money
And my fancy car
You can take my tea
  and honey
And my caviar
You can take away
  my house
And make me live in a hole
But don't you dare
  take away
My rock 'n roll!

Don't you dare take away
My rock 'n roll
Don't you dare take away
My rock 'n roll

Take away my table
Take away my chair
Take away anything—
  I don't care!
But don't you dare
  take away
My rock 'n roll!

You can have my guitar
And my blue suede shoes

You can have my
  hoola-hoop
And my Suzie-Q's
You can take away my T.V.
And my remote control
But don't you dare
  take away
My rock 'n roll

Don't you dare take away
My rock 'n roll
Don't you dare take away
My rock 'n roll

Take my rubber ducky
And my teddy bear
You can take anything—
  I don't care
But don't you dare
  take away
My rock 'n roll!

"R & B"

My kind of music
Comes straight from the heart
Touches your emotions
Right from the start
It speaks of romance
And love so free
It's my favorite kind of music, R & B

When I am singin'
I feel complete
Just like a flower
Lovely and sweet
I see a brand new side of me
With my favorite kind of music, R & B

"R" is for the rhythm that keeps it movin' on
I can move in time with the music all day long
"B" is for the blues when you're feeling down
R & B is the greatest sound around

Once you get the feeling, don't let it go
Let it beat forever deep in your soul
Give yourself a chance now and you will see
That your favorite kind of music is R & B

"Gimme Some Good Ol' Country Music!"

Gimme some good ol'
 country music
With a good ol'
 country beat
You got the rhythm
C'mon and use it
Clappin' and stompin'
 your feet

Just follow that urge
 deep down inside
We all got a little
 country pride
Gimme some good ol'
 country music
And I'll be satisfied!

C'mon now!

Listen to the fiddle!
Hear the guitar play!
You can feel it in
 your middle
Just a little bit
 of country
Goes a long, long way!

Gimme some good ol'
 country music
With a good ol'
 country beat
You got the rhythm
C'mon and use it
Clappin' and stompin'
 your feet

Just follow that urge
 deep down inside
We all got a little
 country pride
Gimme some good ol'
 country music
And I'll be satisfied!

"Any Kind of Music"

Listen to the music, listen to the beat
When we're singing together, ooh the music's sweet

Music! Any kind of music
That's my favorite sound
Music! Any kind of music
Picks you up when you're down

As long as it's got a rhythm
And a catchy melody
Music! Any kind of music
That's all right with me!

Listen to the music, listen to the beat
When we're singing together, ooh the music's sweet!

Music is a language
Reaching out from sea to sea
Music! Any kind of music
That's all right with me!

THE
END